Secrets In My Face

The Whispering Secrets

of

Shinner House

To Pearl
Keep our friendship

By

Ronald Wayne Capodagli, Jr.

ISBN: 978-0-578-93318-4

Dedication

To my wife Jan, your unwavering passion for the written word has been the guiding light that led me on this enchanting journey. Your love for reading has not only shaped your world but has painted the canvas of our shared existence with vibrant hues of imagination and curiosity. Your influence has breathed life into this book, transforming it from mere words to a testament of our connection and the magic that dwells within storytelling.

And to my children, as I pen these words, I envision a future where you will stand on the precipice of parenthood, with your own children beside you, eager to explore the world through the pages of a book. My heart swells with hope that this book will become a cornerstone of your family's story, a bridge that spans generations and carries with it the echo of the past. It is my heartfelt wish that as you read these tales to your children, the flicker of a candle's glow illuminating the words, you will feel the weight of our shared history, the echo of my voice, and the essence of our collective love.

As you lovingly take this book off the shelf, its spine a well-worn companion to your memories, and gently dust off the echoes of time, know that within these pages lie not just a collection of stories, but a vessel of dreams, whispers, and the unspoken bond between us. The stories enclosed hold the magic to inspire, the power to captivate, and the beauty to transcend generations.

With each turning page, as your children lean in closer, their eyes wide with wonder, let their spirits be carried away by the currents of their imagination. Let them wander through the corridors of haunted clocks and ghostly enchantments, discovering the treasure trove of emotions, mysteries, and lessons that these stories hold. May their hearts race with excitement and their minds dance with curiosity, as they, too, become intertwined with the tales woven within.

Let the essence of these stories become the foundation of your family's own tales, stories told around campfires and whispered beneath the covers. May they serve as a catalyst for connection, a lantern guiding your loved ones through the labyrinth of time. Just as I have penned these words for you, my beloved family, may you, in turn, pass on the torch of these stories, lighting the way for generations yet to come.

And so, with the turning of each page, may you find a piece of my heart, a reflection of our shared dreams, and a legacy of love that stretches beyond the confines of time.

Acknowledgment

In the journey of crafting these tales that bridge the realms of the ordinary and the extraordinary, I find myself humbled and grateful for the presence of many souls who have enriched my life with their influence, their stories, and their support.

To my valued customers, your unwavering patience and trust have been the cornerstone of my craft. As I delicately serviced and repaired your "enchanted" clocks, I felt the weight of responsibility and the joy of seeing timepieces return to life, each tick echoing the rhythm of your stories. It has been an honor to be entrusted with these artifacts that hold more than just time – they hold the memories of generations. Your presence in my journey has been a testament to the intricate connections we weave with one another and the stories we share.

To my beloved grandmother, your "scary" stories that you lovingly shared with me during my formative years have left an indelible mark on my soul. Your tales ignited the flames of wonder and curiosity within me, teaching me the art of storytelling, the magic of imagination, and the joy of evoking emotions through words. Your stories have echoed in my heart and found their way onto these pages, intertwining with the ghostly enchantments that have filled my workshop over the years.

To my teachers, I am indebted to your patience and guidance that transformed my daydreams into the art of creative writing. Your nurturing hands shaped my journey, providing me with the tools to paint pictures with words, to weave emotions into sentences, and to create worlds that transcend the confines of reality. Your lessons have been instrumental in transforming my experiences into stories that captivate the imagination and touch the hearts of readers.

Finally, to my cherished wife, your unwavering support and encouragement have been the foundation upon which this book stands. Your belief in my craft, your love for storytelling, and your gentle push during moments of doubt have been my guiding stars. Through the ups and downs of this journey, your presence has been a constant reminder of the power of shared dreams and the magic that blooms when two hearts beat in harmony.

As I pen these words of acknowledgment, I am filled with gratitude for the intricate web of connections that have led me to this point. It is through the threads of relationships, experiences, and shared moments that these stories have come to life. Each page, each word, carries within it the essence of those who have touched my life, and I am privileged to share their essence with the world.

With a heart brimming with appreciation and a pen dipped in gratitude, I offer my acknowledgments to all who have walked this path with me. May these stories be a tribute to the bonds that unite us, the stories that define us, and the enchantments that make life a tapestry of wonder.

About The Author

Ronald Wayne Capodagli, Jr., a man with a lifetime dedicated to the meticulous craft of clockmaking, had become more than just a skilled craftsman; he was a keeper of time, an artisan of history, and a witness to the mysteries that lurked beyond the ticking hands. With four decades of experience under his belt, Ronald's hands had shaped, repaired, and brought to life an array of clocks that spanned generations.

In the quiet solitude of his workshop, where the air was scented with the fragrance of wood and the gentle rhythm of ticking echoed, Ronald had honed his craft with an unwavering dedication to excellence. Each clock that passed through his hands was not merely a mechanical marvel; it was a testament to his passion, his artistry, and his commitment to raising the standards of craftsmanship.

Yet, as the years went by and Ronald's reputation as a master clockmaker grew, he discovered that there was a dimension to his work that transcended the realm of gears and springs. Behind the intricate mechanisms and polished wood, he began to sense a presence – a whisper of something otherworldly. It was as though the very essence of time itself had woven its magic into the fibers of the clocks he crafted and repaired.

With a mixture of awe and curiosity, Ronald realized that his workshop had become a haven not only for the craftsmanship he had perfected but also for the lingering spirits of the past. Ghostly enchantments, as he came to call them, were occurrences that defied logical explanation – the soft rustle of a fabric in an empty room, the faint tinkling of laughter that seemed to linger in the air, and the inexplicable chime of a clock that had long fallen silent.

It was these ghostly enchantments that compelled Ronald to put pen to paper, to share the stories that had unfolded in the quiet corners of his workshop throughout the years. In his book, he sought to peel back the veneer of his craft, revealing the hidden layers of mystery and magic that had become an integral part of the clocks he had come to know so intimately.

With each page turned, readers would be invited into Ronald's world – a world where the passage of time blurred the boundaries between the tangible and the ethereal. He chronicled the moments when he had felt a presence that couldn't be explained, when clocks seemed to come alive with a spirit of their own, and when the stories of their previous owners whispered through the hands of time.

Through his words, Ronald would take his readers on a journey beyond the mechanics of clockmaking, into a realm where history and the supernatural converged. He would recount the tale of an antique grandfather clock that chimed on a moonless night, resonating with a melody that had been lost to time. He would share the story of a pocket watch that seemed to slow down whenever a storm was brewing, as if echoing the heartbeat of the tempest itself.

In crafting his book, Ronald realized that his legacy as a clockmaker extended beyond the ticking of gears and the precision of his hands. He was a storyteller, a weaver of narratives that bridged the gap between the known and the unknown. His book would be a testament to the fact that there was more to a clock than its mechanics – there was a soul, a history, and a connection to the mysteries of the universe.

As he penned his experiences, Ronald felt a sense of fulfillment. He had spent a lifetime raising the standards of excellence in his craft, and now he was raising the veil that separated the ordinary from the extraordinary. His book would be a tribute to the ghostly enchantments that had become an inseparable part of his clockmaking journey, and a gift to those who dared to listen to the echoes of time and the whispers of the beyond.

Preface

Welcome to the pages of "Secrets in My Face," a collection of chilling tales that will send shivers down your spine and make you question the very essence of time. Within these stories lie the secrets that clocks have guarded for generations, the mysteries that have lingered in the shadows, waiting to be unveiled. These tales are not merely stories; they are gateways to a world where the ordinary and the supernatural collide, where the ticking of a clock can become a symphony of haunting melodies.

As you embark on this journey through the unknown, prepare to encounter a selection of short stories that will transport you to the heart of the eerie and the unexplained. The clocks in these tales hold more than just the measurement of hours – they harbor whispers of history, echoes of forgotten lives, and spirits yearning to break free or be heeded.

You may never look at clocks in the same way again.

The allure of timepieces has always been their ability to measure the passage of moments. However, beneath their polished surfaces lies a world of secrets and stories that defy the rational and embrace the enigmatic. From the gentle ticking of a grandfather clock to the echoing chimes of a haunted mantel clock, each tale invites you to peer into the hidden realms where time and the supernatural intertwine.

As you read these stories, you'll find yourself drawn into the depths of each haunting narrative. You'll traverse through the corridors of time, where apparitions lurk in the corners, and whispers from the past find their way into the present. You'll witness the power of the human imagination as it conjures both fear and fascination, blurring the lines between reality and the unknown.

And, of course, you'll discover that bedtime, once a time of rest and dreams, can transform into an hour of anticipation and chills. As you turn off the lights and settle under your covers, the stories within this collection will accompany you, inviting you to journey into the realms of the supernatural, where clocks become vessels of both the mundane and the mystical.

So, dear reader, as you prepare to dive into the pages of "Secrets in My Face," be ready to unlock the secrets that clocks hold within their ticking hearts. Embrace the shivers, the gasps, and the sense of wonder that these stories will evoke. And when you glance at a clock, whether it be during daylight hours or the hushed moments of night, remember that time is not always as straightforward as it seems.

The clocks house secrets, the spirits within yearn to be released or obeyed, and the tales you are about to experience will linger in your thoughts long after you've turned the final page. Are you ready to explore the unknown, to venture into the realm of the supernatural, and to encounter the secrets that lie hidden in the face of time? Then turn the page, and let the journey begin.

Chapter 1

The Enchanted

Long ago, in the heart of the southern countryside, there stood a magnificent oak tree. This oak had witnessed the rise and fall of civilizations, the passing of generations, and the telling of countless tales. Its sturdy branches provided shelter to explorers, its leaves whispered secrets to the wind, and its roots absorbed the stories of the land. This ancient oak was not just a tree; it was a silent keeper of the South's most intriguing tales.

The Whispering Secrets of Shinner House

As time went by, the tree's reputation spread far and wide. Legends grew around its magical properties, and people journeyed from distant lands to seek its wisdom. Among those who ventured to the oak were two explorers, Kelly and Skippy, who were known for their daring expeditions and insatiable curiosity.

Kelly and Skippy had heard stories of the oak's enchantment, of how it could grant wishes to those who understood its secrets. Determined to uncover the truth, they embarked on a journey to find the tree. After a long and challenging expedition, they finally reached the ancient oak.

The tree sensed the explorers' respect for its history and their genuine curiosity. It revealed itself to them in a burst of ethereal light, and a bond was formed. In gratitude for their reverence, the oak shared its magic with Kelly and Skippy, allowing them to carve a piece of its wood to create a grand masterpiece – a grandfather clock that would stand as a testament to their adventure.

The wood of the oak was carefully crafted into the clock's intricate design, with carvings that told the stories of the South's history and the oak's own journey through time. As the clock took shape, Kelly and Skippy realized that the tree's magic had woven itself into the wood, infusing it with a power they could hardly comprehend.

The Whispering Secrets of Shinner House

Upon completing the clock, Kelly and Skippy realized that the true source of the tree's magic was not just in granting wishes, but in fostering a deep connection to the past, a respect for nature, and a sense of responsibility for the future. The clock's enchantment reflected the tree's spirit, a bridge between generations, and a guardian of the South's most intriguing tales.

The clock was placed in their estate, Shinner House, which became a hub of activity during a time when explorers were celebrated for their daring expeditions and insatiable curiosity. Generations ago, Kelly and Skippy had embarked on journeys to far-off lands, returning with exotic treasures, artifacts, and tales that fueled the imaginations of the townspeople for decades.

And so, the grandfather clock made from the 200-year-old oak tree became not just a timekeeper, but a storyteller, a reminder of the past's rich tapestry, and a guide to shaping a better future. Its enchantment whispered tales of the South's history, its melodies carried the wisdom of the ages, and its presence continued to inspire those who gazed upon it.

Through the clock, the oak's magic lived on, touching the lives of those who recognized the power of history, the value of stories, and the importance of cherishing the world around them. As time marched forward, the clock's enchantment remained, a timeless echo of the ancient oak's enduring legacy.

The Whispering Secrets of Shinner House

Kelly: (Gazing at the ancient oak in awe) Skippy, can you believe we've finally found it? The legendary oak with its rumored enchantment.

Skippy: (Equally amazed) It's more breathtaking than I imagined. The stories were true – this tree holds a power beyond our understanding.

Kelly: (Approaching the oak with reverence) I can feel its presence, Skippy. It's as if this oak has witnessed the history of the South itself.

Skippy: (Running his hand over the oak's bark) And now, it's granting us the chance to be a part of that history. To leave our mark on its legacy.

Kelly: (Looking at the carving tools in their hands) We should do this with utmost respect. We're not just taking wood from a tree; we're taking a piece of its essence.

Skippy: (Nodding) You're right, Kelly. We need to approach this with reverence and gratitude. This tree has shown us its magic, and it's an honor to be entrusted with it.

Kelly: (Beginning to carve the wood) As we shape this wood into something new, let's remember the journeys that brought us here. The explorations, the challenges, the wonders we've seen.

Skippy: (Carving alongside Kelly) And let's also remember the stories this tree holds – the tales of those who stood beneath its branches, the generations it has watched over.

Kelly: (As the carving takes shape) This wood will become a symbol of our adventure, a testament to our curiosity and determination.

Skippy: (Finishing his carving) And when we're done, we'll have created not just a clock, but a masterpiece that carries the magic of this oak with it.

Kelly: (Admiring their work) Look at it, Skippy. Our very own grandfather clock, infused with the spirit of the oak.

Skippy: (Gazing at the clock with pride) It's a connection to the past, a link to the stories that have unfolded under this tree's watchful gaze.

Kelly: (Placing a hand on the clock) The clock will continue to tell tales, to whisper its melodies, just like this oak has done for centuries.

Skippy: (Smiling) And as the clock's hands tick forward, let's remember the journey that brought us here, and the magical bond we share with this tree.

The Whispering Secrets of Shinner House

Kelly: (With a sense of wonder) We are part of its story now, Skippy. Our adventure will echo through time, just like the tales it's carried for generations.

Skippy: (Taking a step back, looking at the clock and the oak) Our legacy intertwined with the legacy of this oak – it's a beautiful connection, Kelly.

Kelly: (Sharing a moment of reflection) Let's treasure this bond, Skippy, and let the clock remind us of the magic we've discovered and the stories we've become a part of.

As they stand before the newly carved clock, Kelly and Skippy share a moment of unity, grateful for the opportunity to create a masterpiece that would carry the oak's magic and their own adventurous spirit into the future.

Chapter 2

The Mysterious Inheritance

In the heart of the charming town of Hutto, three sisters – Gemma, Harley, and Jolie – found themselves inheriting an old estate known as Shinner House. The house held a captivating history, once owned by the Boomer family, Kelly and Skippy, and it was said to be home to an enchanted grandfather clock made from a 200-year-old tree that had seen the South's most intriguing tales.

The Whispering Secrets of Shinner House

Shinner House held a captivating history that unfolded like pages from an old, treasured book. Once owned by the Boomer family, Kelly and Skippy, the estate had been a hub of activity during a time when explorers were celebrated for their daring expeditions and insatiable curiosity. Generations ago, the Boomer family, Kelly and Skippy had embarked on journeys to far-off lands, returning with exotic treasures, artifacts, and tales that had fueled the imaginations of the townspeople for decades.

At the heart of the estate's legend was the enchanted grandfather clock. Crafted from the wood of a majestic oak tree that had stood for over two centuries in the heart of the deep South, the clock bore intricate carvings that told stories of times long past. This ancient tree had borne witness to the region's most intriguing tales – from the whispered secrets of hidden coves to the bustling life of a bustling riverfront town. Its rings held echoes of laughter, whispers of lovers' promises, and the haunting cries of farewell.

The sisters were no strangers to tales of adventure and magic, having grown up on the stories of explorations passed down through their family. With their unique blend of wonder, curiosity, and determination, they embraced the opportunity to unearth the estate's secrets. From the moment they set foot inside Shinner House, they felt the presence of those who had walked its halls before them –

The Whispering Secrets of Shinner House

adventurers who had left behind traces of their journeys in the form of maps, journals, and artifacts.

As Gemma, the eldest sister, delved into dusty records and archives, she unearthed journals that chronicled Kelly and Skippy's travels. She discovered faded maps that hinted at hidden treasures within the estate's sprawling gardens, triggering her sense of leadership and duty to preserve her family's legacy.

Harley, the middle sister with an artist's soul, found herself captivated by the clock's intricate carvings. With each swirl and curl of the wood, she felt a connection to the artists who had poured their creativity into the timeless masterpiece. As she spent hours sketching the clock, its stories seemed to come alive before her eyes, igniting her imagination and filling her mind with a world of possibility.

And then there was Jolie, the youngest of the trio, whose heart resonated deeply with the whispers of the old oak tree. She spent her days beneath its gnarled branches, feeling a sense of kinship with the past and a longing for the companionship of the spirits that seemed to linger. Jolie's unwavering belief in the magic of the estate drew her into a world where the boundaries between reality and fantasy blurred, and where she could almost hear the laughter of explorers and the rustling of crinoline skirts.

Together, the sisters embarked on a journey of discovery, each following her own path while collectively uncovering

The Whispering Secrets of Shinner House

the estate's hidden treasures and untold stories. As they ventured deeper into the heart of Shinner House, they began to unravel the intertwined destinies of their ancestors and the clock that held the key to bridging the past and present.

With every turn of the clock's golden hands, the enchantment of the estate grew stronger. The melodies it played were not just tunes but echoes of adventures, promises, and dreams that had once filled its halls. The sisters felt a powerful connection to the explorers who had roamed these very rooms and to the enchanted tree that had witnessed their exploits.

As the sisters uncovered the clock's secrets — compartments that held maps, keys, and enchanted objects — they found themselves drawn into a tapestry woven with threads of history, magic, and family bonds. Their individual quests intertwined like vines, creating a story that celebrated their strengths, passions, and the unbreakable bond between sisters.

And so, within the walls of Shinner House, where the past and present danced in harmony, Gemma, Harley, and Jolie embarked on a journey that would forever intertwine their lives with the legacy of Kelly and Skippy. Through their determination, courage, and unwavering belief in the extraordinary, they would unlock the true magic of the enchanted grandfather clock, discovering that the most enchanting tales are those that are shared across generations, connecting hearts and minds in a timeless dance of wonder and adventure.

Gemma: (Excitedly exploring Shinner House) Can you believe it, you two? This is our house now, our legacy!

Harley: (Looking around in awe) I know, Gemma. It's like stepping into a fairy tale. And did you hear about that enchanted grandfather clock?

Jolie: (Curious) Yeah, I heard. They say it's made from a 200-year-old tree and holds the stories of the South. How cool is that?

Gemma: (Grinning) It's like the heart of this place beats with all the history and magic of generations past.

Harley: (Walking over to the clock, running her fingers along its edges) Just think about all the stories it could tell. The people who walked through these halls, the celebrations, the secrets...

Jolie: (Looking thoughtful) And the Boomer family, Kelly and Skippy who once owned this house. Can you imagine the adventures they must have had?

The Whispering Secrets of Shinner House

Gemma: (Enthusiastic) I bet they had the most incredible journeys. I've always loved hearing stories about explorers and their daring expeditions.

Harley: (Smirking) Gemma, you're already planning our own explorations, aren't you?

Gemma: (Laughing) Well, who knows what we might discover in this old estate? Maybe there's a hidden treasure waiting for us.

Jolie: (Teasingly) Or maybe just a bunch of old antiques.

Gemma: (Playful) Hey, antiques can be valuable too! But seriously, I can't wait to make our own mark on Shinner House, just like the Boomer family, Kelly and Skippy did.

Harley: (Nodding) Yeah, and who knows? Maybe one day, someone will be talking about the adventures of Gemma, Harley, and Jolie.

Jolie: (Dreamy) Wouldn't that be something? To know that our stories and experiences become a part of this place's history.

Gemma: (Squeezing their hands) Sisters, we're embarking on a new chapter together. Let's make it as memorable and magical as the tales this house holds.

Harley: (Looking at the clock again) And who knows? Maybe that enchanted clock will whisper its stories to us as we create our own.

The Whispering Secrets of Shinner House

Jolie: (Smiling) Well then, here's to embracing the history and magic of Shinner House, and to writing our own stories that will echo through the years.

They raise their hands in a sisterly toast, their excitement and determination filling the air.

Chapter 3

The Tree's Secret Song

The sisters soon discovered the enchanted grandfather clock, its polished wood and delicate chimes drawing them in. The clock had been crafted from a tree with a sordid past, and its intricate carvings whispered secrets of the deep South. As moonlight bathed the clock, it would softly sing a haunting melody that seemed to tell stories of days long gone.

The Whispering Secrets of Shinner House

The sisters, fueled by their curiosity and a sense of destiny, explored the nooks and crannies of Shinner House. One day, as they wandered deeper into the heart of the estate, they stumbled upon a room that seemed to emanate an aura of ancient wisdom. At its center stood the enchanted grandfather clock, a masterpiece that held the essence of the tree's sorted past.

The clock's polished wood gleamed in the soft sunlight that filtered through the room's lace-draped windows. Its surface was adorned with intricate carvings that depicted scenes of the old South, capturing moments of grace, adventure, and mystery. As if etched by the hands of time itself, the carvings told stories of grand plantation parties, moonlit riverboat excursions, and whispered conversations beneath magnolia trees. The clock had been crafted with care, its wood resonating with the spirit of the ancient oak tree that had witnessed centuries of change.

Drawn to the clock's allure, the sisters reached out to touch its smooth surface. They could feel a gentle hum beneath their fingertips, as if the clock held a heartbeat of its own, synced with the rhythm of the past. The delicate chimes that hung from its golden frame tinkled softly in response, like a melody that only the clock could hear.

The clock's secrets were not easily revealed. It was as though each carving held a piece of the puzzle, a key to unlocking the stories that had been etched into its very being. Gemma, with her penchant for leadership and exploration, traced the carvings with her finger, deciphering hidden patterns that seemed to guide her towards a hidden compartment.

With a soft click, the compartment was revealed, and inside lay a bundle of aged parchment. The sisters gingerly unrolled the parchment, revealing a map that detailed the estate's sprawling gardens. The map was unlike any they had ever seen, marked with symbols that hinted at hidden treasures and enchanted pathways.

As night descended upon the estate, bathing it in the silvery glow of the moon, the clock's true magic began to unfurl. The room seemed to come alive with a soft luminescence, and the clock's chimes took on a haunting, ethereal quality. As the moonlight kissed the clock's surface, it would softly sing a haunting melody that seemed to transcend time itself.

The melody was a whisper from the past, a lament that told of love found and lost, of dreams chased and forsaken. It carried the weight of history, and its notes resonated with the heartache and joy of generations gone by. As the clock sang its mournful tune, the room transformed into a portal, allowing the sisters to step into the scenes depicted in its carvings.

They danced at grand plantation balls, their dresses swishing as they twirled beneath crystal chandeliers. They navigated moonlit riverboat excursions, feeling the cool

The Whispering Secrets of Shinner House

breeze on their skin as they glided along the water's surface. They eavesdropped on whispered conversations beneath magnolia trees, their hearts fluttering with the promise of secret rendezvous.

With each journey into the past, the sisters felt a deep connection to the history that had shaped their family and their beloved estate. They learned that the clock was not merely a timekeeper, but a bridge between the present and the past, a conduit through which they could experience the lives and stories of those who had come before them.

As dawn broke and the melody faded into the ether, the sisters gathered around the clock, their hearts full of wonder and gratitude. The clock's carvings seemed to glow with a newfound luminosity, as if the stories it held had been given new life through their experiences. The sisters realized that the clock was not just a relic of the past; it was a living testament to the enduring power of history, the magic of family, and the threads that bound their lives to those who had walked the halls of Shinner House long ago.

And so, with the enchantment of the grandfather clock as their guide, the sisters continued to explore the hidden depths of Shinner House, uncovering the layers of history that intertwined their lives with the legacy of the past. Each delicate chime, each haunting melody, was a reminder that time was not just a linear progression, but a tapestry woven with stories that spanned generations, connecting the sisters to a world of wonder and mystery that had been waiting to be rediscovered.

Gemma: (Gazing at the enchanted grandfather clock) This is it, the legendary clock. It's even more beautiful than I imagined.

Harley: (Running her fingers along the carvings) Look at the details on this wood. It's like every inch holds a piece of history.

Jolie: (Listening to the delicate chimes) And did you hear that? The chimes have this... ethereal quality.

Gemma: (Excited) They say this clock was made from a tree with a sorted past. Imagine all the secrets it holds.

Harley: (Mesmerized) And the carvings, they seem to be telling a story. Look, here's a scene of a river, and there's a figure that looks like a Southern belle.

Jolie: (Lost in thought) It's like the clock is whispering to us, sharing glimpses of the deep South's history.

Gemma: (As moonlight bathes the clock) And when the moonlight touches it, it's like it comes alive.

The Whispering Secrets of Shinner House

Harley: (Listening to the haunting melody) Do you hear that? The clock is softly singing, like a ghostly lullaby.

Jolie: (Reflective) It's like the clock is singing the stories of days long gone, of people who lived and loved in this house.

Gemma: (Smiling) Maybe it's telling the tales of the Boomer family, Kelly and Skippy, and the explorations they embarked on.

Harley: (Dreamy) Or maybe it's sharing the moments of joy and laughter that echoed through these walls during the grand parties they hosted.

Jolie: (Sighing contentedly) I feel a deep connection to this clock, to this house. It's like we're becoming a part of its story too.

Gemma: (Linking their hands together) Sisters, as we embrace Shinner House and all its history, we're also creating our own stories.

Harley: (Looking at the clock with determination) And just like the clock's carvings, our lives will have intricate and meaningful moments.

Jolie: (Listening to the clock's melody) Let's remember this night, the night we discovered the heart of Shinner House.

The Whispering Secrets of Shinner House

Gemma: (In agreement) And as the clock sings its haunting melody, let's remember that we're adding our voices to the chorus of stories it holds.

They stand together in the moonlit room, their bond and shared sense of purpose growing stronger as the clock's gentle melody weaves through their thoughts.

Chapter 4

Gemma's Discovery

Gemma, the eldest sister, was an adventurer at heart. One night, she heard the clock's melody grow stronger, leading her to a hidden compartment within. Inside, she found a letter from Kelly and Skippy, describing the tree's magic and how it had granted them wishes. Gemma was determined to uncover the truth behind the tree's powers.

The Whispering Secrets of Shinner House

Gemma, the eldest sister, possessed an unquenchable thirst for adventure. Her heartbeat was in rhythm with the tales of explorers and pioneers who had dared to venture into the unknown. From a young age, she had poured over maps, tracing the paths of those who had left their mark on history. Her room was adorned with artifacts and trinkets, each telling a story of a distant land and a daring journey.

One fateful night, as the moon cast its silvery glow over Shinner House, Gemma lay awake in her bed, captivated by the haunting melody that emanated from the grandfather clock. The notes seemed to resonate with her very soul, pulling her from the confines of her room. Guided by the enchanting music, she followed its siren call through the moonlit halls, her steps light and purposeful.

The melody grew stronger, leading her to a room that felt different from the others. It was as if the walls themselves were alive with an energy that reached out to her. The clock stood at the center of the room, its polished wood aglow in the moonlight. Gemma approached it with a mixture of anticipation and reverence, her fingers brushing the surface of its carvings.

As if in response to her touch, a soft click echoed through the room, and a hidden compartment was revealed. Inside lay a delicate envelope, its paper aged and yellowed with time. With trembling hands, Gemma carefully unfolded the letter within. The words on the page were penned by none

The Whispering Secrets of Shinner House

other than Kelly and Skippy, the adventurers who had once called Shinner House their home.

The letter described the tree from which the clock had been crafted – a tree that had stood for centuries as a silent witness to the deep South's most enchanting tales. Kelly and Skippy's words painted a vivid picture of their encounters with the tree's magic, a magic that had granted them wishes beyond their wildest dreams. They spoke of moonlit nights when the tree would come alive with soft whispers and glimmering lights, a phenomenon they could only attribute to the ancient oak's mystical powers.

Gemma's heart raced as she read on, her mind ablaze with questions and possibilities. The letter spoke of the tree's connection to the clock, how its essence had been woven into the very fabric of the timepiece. Kelly and Skippy had discovered that the clock possessed the ability to channel the tree's magic, its melodies serving as a conduit between the past and the present.

Intrigued and determined, Gemma resolved to uncover the truth behind the tree's powers. She studied the letter's descriptions of the tree's location, its distinctive markings, and the rituals that Kelly and Skippy had performed to harness its magic. Armed with this newfound knowledge, she set out to retrace their steps and rediscover the hidden grove that had been the source of so much wonder.

The Whispering Secrets of Shinner House

Days turned into nights as Gemma ventured deep into the estate's gardens, guided by the moonlight and the memories etched within the letter. She followed the twists and turns of the old map, her heart pounding with anticipation as she approached the sacred grove described by her ancestors.

And then, there it was – a gnarled and majestic oak tree, its branches reaching towards the sky like the outstretched arms of an ancient guardian. As the moonlight bathed the tree in its silvery glow, Gemma felt a surge of energy, a connection that seemed to bridge the gap between past and present. The tree whispered to her with a voice woven from the winds that had blown through its branches for centuries.

With the letter's guidance, Gemma performed the rituals that had been described – the whispered words, the offering of a single golden leaf, the deep connection to the magic of the South. And then, as if responding to her call, the tree's energy pulsed around her, wrapping her in a cocoon of warmth and wonder.

As she stood beneath the ancient oak, Gemma felt a surge of determination and purpose. The tree's magic was real, and it held the power to grant wishes, just as it had done for Kelly and Skippy. She closed her eyes and made her wish, her heart overflowing with hope and longing.

The Whispering Secrets of Shinner House

In that moment, as the tree's energy enveloped her, Gemma understood that the magic of Shinner House was not just a tale of the past, but a living, breathing force that connected her to her family's legacy and to the mysteries of the deep South. With the clock as her guide and the tree's magic as her companion, she was ready to embrace the adventure that lay ahead, determined to uncover the truth, and unlock the tree's powers for herself.

And so, Gemma's journey had only just begun, fueled by the whispers of the past, the enchantment of the present, and the promise of a future woven with magic, wonder, and the unbreakable bond of family.

Gemma: (Excitedly entering the room) You won't believe what happened last night. I heard the clock's melody grow so strong, it was like it was calling out to me.

Harley: (Curious) Calling out? What do you mean?

Jolie: (Intrigued) Yeah, Gemma, what happened?

Gemma: (Eagerly) I followed the sound, and it led me to the clock. But then, I noticed something unusual – a hidden compartment in the base.

The Whispering Secrets of Shinner House

Harley: (Surprised) A hidden compartment? This is getting mysterious.

Jolie: (Wide-eyed) What was inside?

Gemma: (Holding up a letter) This letter. It's from none other than Kelly and Skippy, the explorers who once owned this house.

Jolie: (Excited) What does it say?

Gemma: (Reading aloud) "To the soul who unlocks this compartment, you've uncovered the heart of Shinner House's magic. The clock's wood was crafted from a tree that held ancient powers, granting wishes to those who understood its secrets."

Harley: (In awe) Wishes? Like, real wishes?

Gemma: (Nodding) They believed the tree had a connection to the deep South's magic, and they wrote that it granted them their greatest wishes.

Jolie: (Thoughtful) So, you mean to say that this clock, made from that magical tree, has the power to grant wishes?

Gemma: (Determined) I think so. And I want to find out for sure. Imagine the possibilities if we could harness this magic for good.

Harley: (Skeptical) But how do we know it's not just a story? I mean, magic trees and wishes?

The Whispering Secrets of Shinner House

Gemma: (Looking resolute) Kelly and Skippy weren't the type to spin tall tales. And the way the clock's melody guided me to the letter... it felt like the clock itself was urging us to uncover its secret.

Jolie: (Nodding) I'm with you, Gemma. This could be our chance to make a real impact, to fulfill our own dreams and maybe even help others along the way.

Gemma: (Grinning) That's exactly what I was thinking. I want us to explore this further, to uncover the truth behind the tree's magic and learn how we can use it to make a difference.

Harley: (Relenting) Okay, count me in. Let's dive into the mysteries of this clock and see where it leads us.

Jolie: (Excited) Sisters on an adventure to unlock the magic of Shinner House. Who would have thought?

With their determination set, the sisters stand united, ready to embark on a new chapter filled with exploration, magic, and the possibility of wishes coming true.

Chapter 5

Harley's Artistic Connection

Harley, with her passion for art, discovered that her paintings seemed to come alive when placed near the clock. The tree's spirit infused her artwork, bringing it to life with vibrant colors and moving scenes. She realized that the clock's magic had a profound connection to creativity, inspiring her to create a gallery of enchanted paintings.

The Whispering Secrets of Shinner House

Harley, with her heart full of creativity and her mind brimming with imagination, often found solace in the corners of Shinner House where sunlight filtered through leaded windows and cast dancing patterns upon the aged wooden floorboards. Her room was a haven of colors and canvases, with brushes and palettes strewn about like confetti at a celebration of art. Each stroke of her brush was a story waiting to be told, a world waiting to be explored.

One quiet afternoon, when the sunlight slanted through the window at an angle that seemed almost magical, Harley set her latest canvas upon an easel near the enchanting grandfather clock. With every brushstroke, she poured her emotions onto the canvas, infusing it with the stories and dreams that swirled within her heart. The melody of the clock's chimes resonated in the air, a harmonious backdrop to her creative endeavors.

As she painted, something extraordinary began to happen. The vibrant colors seemed to come alive, shifting and blending in ways she had never seen before. It was as though the very essence of the clock's magic had woven itself into her artwork, breathing life into her strokes and giving birth to scenes that danced and twirled with a vitality that defied explanation.

In awe, Harley watched as the characters she had painted leapt from the canvas, their movements fluid and graceful. The landscapes she had imagined stretched and expanded,

The Whispering Secrets of Shinner House

taking on a breathtaking depth that drew her into their embrace. Birds took flight, flowers swayed in an unseen breeze, and rivers shimmered with a life of their own. It was a realm of enchantment and wonder, a world where her creations stepped beyond the boundaries of the canvas and into reality.

With wide eyes and a heart pounding with exhilaration, Harley experimented further. She painted a lively market scene, and as she placed it near the clock, the bustling crowd seemed to buzz with a newfound energy. She painted a serene woodland glade, and the leaves rustled as though touched by a breeze only they could feel. She painted a starlit sky, and the stars twinkled with a brilliance that mirrored the night sky itself.

With each painting, Harley discovered that the clock's magic had a profound connection to creativity. It was as though the ancient oak's spirit had intertwined with her artistic endeavors, granting her the ability to give life to her creations. Her gallery of enchanted paintings grew, each piece telling a story that transcended the limits of paint and canvas.

Word of Harley's remarkable art spread throughout the town of Hutto, drawing curious visitors to the estate. They marveled at her gallery, where scenes of fantasy and reality merged in a symphony of color and motion. Children laughed as they reached out to touch the petals of a flower that seemed to bloom beneath their fingertips,

The Whispering Secrets of Shinner House

and adults stared in awe as they witnessed a waterfall cascading down a canvas with a lifelike grace.

Harley's artistic journey became a testament to the power of imagination, the beauty of collaboration between the natural world and the human spirit. Her gallery became a sanctuary of inspiration, a place where dreams could be touched, and stories could be experienced in ways that were beyond the ordinary.

As the days turned into nights, and the enchanting melodies of the clock continued to weave their spell, Harley's passion for art deepened. She realized that the magic of the clock had opened a doorway to a realm where the boundaries between reality and fantasy blurred, and where creativity held the power to shape the world around her.

With each stroke of her brush, Harley painted not only on canvas but on the very fabric of the estate itself. She became a conduit for the clock's magic, allowing the spirit of the ancient oak to dance through her fingertips and breathe life into her art. Her gallery became a testament to the intertwining of creativity and enchantment, a living testament to the extraordinary stories that could be told when imagination and magic joined hands.

And so, within the halls of Shinner House, where the ancient oak's spirit whispered through the leaves and the clock's melodies sang of tales long gone, Harley's gallery of enchanted paintings became a celebration of the wondrous dance between art and life, where dreams took flight and the ordinary transformed into the extraordinary.

Gemma: (Entering the room, finding Harley absorbed in her art) There you are, Harley. What's got you so focused?

Harley: (Looking up, a wide smile on her face) Gemma, Jolie, you won't believe this. Look at this painting.

Jolie: (Curious, approaching the painting) It's beautiful, Harley. Your art has always been amazing.

Gemma: (Admiring the painting) It's definitely stunning, but what's so special about it?

Harley: (Excitedly) Watch this. (She picks up the painting and places it near the clock.)

Jolie: (Watching as the painting seems to come alive) Whoa, did you see that?

Gemma: (Amazed) The waterfall is actually moving, and the colors are so vibrant.

Harley: (Grinning) The clock's magic is infusing my artwork with life. It's like the tree's spirit is interacting with my paintings.

The Whispering Secrets of Shinner House

Jolie: (Looking at the clock in awe) It's as if the clock isn't just a timekeeper; it's a source of inspiration.

Gemma: (Realizing) So, the clock's magic is connected to creativity. It's not just about wishes, but about bringing art to life.

Harley: (Nodding) Exactly. The stories, the emotions, they're all coming alive on canvas. This is the power of the tree's magic.

Jolie: (Thoughtful) It's like the clock wants to continue the legacy of the Boomer family, Kelly and Skippy – their love for exploration and creativity.

Gemma: (Looking at Harley's painting) You know what this means, right?

Harley: (Excited) It means I have to create more. An entire gallery of enchanted paintings, each telling its own story.

Jolie: (Enthusiastic) And people from all around could come to experience the magic of your art.

Gemma: (Grinning) Shinner House could become known for not only its history but also as a haven for creativity and inspiration.

Harley: (Fired up) Let's do it. Let's create a gallery that captures the heart of the clock's magic and share it with the world.

The Whispering Secrets of Shinner House

Jolie: (Agreeing) The stories told through your art could inspire others to find their own creativity and passions.

Gemma: (With determination) Sisters, let's embrace the full scope of Shinner House's magic. We have wishes to uncover and stories to tell.

Harley: (Excited) And art to bring to life like never before.

Jolie: (Looking at the clock) Our journey has only just begun, and the canvas of our future is waiting to be painted with the colors of adventure and magic.

With renewed purpose, the sisters gather their ideas and enthusiasm, ready to create a gallery that not only captures the essence of the clock's magic but also becomes a beacon of inspiration for all who visit.

Chapter 6

Jolie's Curiosity

Jolie, the youngest sister, was curious about the clock's past. With the help of the town's historian, she learned about the tree's origins and the people it had touched. Through old photographs and journals, she uncovered stories of love, adventure, and dreams that had been influenced by the tree's enchantment.

The Whispering Secrets of Shinner House

Jolie, the youngest of the sisters, possessed a curiosity that burned like a candle in the darkness, lighting her path towards the hidden corners of Shinner House. While her elder sisters explored the clock's melodies and paintings, Jolie found herself drawn to the stories that lay dormant in the estate's archives, waiting to be rediscovered.

One sunny morning, with a determined glint in her eyes, Jolie set out to unravel the secrets of the clock's past. She sought out the town's historian, an elderly gentleman named Mr. Cooper, known for his encyclopedic knowledge of Hutto's history. Armed with a notebook and a pen, Jolie listened with rapt attention as Mr. Cooper regaled her with tales of the ancient oak tree that had been the source of the clock's wood.

With a mixture of fascination and respect, Mr. Cooper told her of the tree's origins, tracing its history back over two centuries. He spoke of how the tree had been a silent witness to the rise and fall of the South's most captivating stories, from grand plantation parties to whispered conversations beneath its branches.

Guided by Mr. Cooper's wisdom, Jolie delved deeper into the estate's archives. Dusty photographs and delicate journals transported her back in time, offering glimpses of the people who had walked the halls of Shinner House and felt the touch of the tree's magic. As she pored over old albums, she saw couples dancing at lavish balls, their laughter echoing through the ages. She read letters

The Whispering Secrets of Shinner House

exchanged between star-crossed lovers, their words dripping with tenderness and longing.

One journal in particular captured Jolie's heart – a diary kept by a young woman named Arya, who had lived in the estate during a time when the South was a tapestry of tradition and transformation. Arya's words painted a vivid portrait of her daily life, her dreams, and the moments she had shared with a kindred spirit beneath the ancient oak.

Through Arya's diary, Jolie discovered that the tree had been a silent confidant to generations of lovers. It had borne witness to whispered promises and stolen glances, offering a sanctuary where hearts could beat in rhythm with the secrets of the heart. The tree's enchantment had a way of weaving itself into these stories, bestowing a touch of magic upon every stolen kiss and every heartfelt vow.

Inspired by Arya's story and the countless others she uncovered, Jolie realized that the clock was more than just a conduit for melodies and paintings – it was a keeper of memories, a vessel that held the collective dreams of those who had passed through Shinner House. The clock's haunting melodies were a chorus of voices from the past, echoing through the corridors of time.

Driven by her newfound understanding, Jolie began to curate a collection of stories that paid homage to the tree's influence on the lives it had touched. She meticulously

The Whispering Secrets of Shinner House

documented each tale, weaving a tapestry of love, adventure, and dreams that showcased the tree's profound connection to the people who had once sought solace beneath its branches.

With the guidance of Mr. Cooper, Jolie organized a special exhibit within the estate, transforming one of its rooms into a gallery of memories. Framed photographs, excerpts from journals, and snippets of love letters adorned the walls, each capturing a moment frozen in time, a fragment of the tree's legacy.

Visitors to the estate were captivated by Jolie's exhibit, drawn into the stories that whispered through the photographs and danced in the air. Children listened with wide eyes as their parents recounted tales of their own ancestors who had been part of Shinner House's history. Couples held hands and gazed at the photographs of lovers who had found each other beneath the tree's protective branches.

Jolie's exhibit became a testament to the enduring power of the tree's enchantment, a bridge between the past and the present, and a celebration of the timeless stories that were woven into the fabric of Shinner House. Through her tireless efforts, Jolie ensured that the memory of those who had been touched by the tree's magic would live on, inspiring generations to come with tales of love, courage, and the enduring spirit of a place where dreams took root and flourished.

The Whispering Secrets of Shinner House

And so, within the heart of Shinner House, where the clock's melodies wove their enchantment and the paintings danced with life, Jolie's exhibit stood as a tribute to the tree's legacy and a reminder that the past was not just a distant memory, but a living treasure waiting to be discovered by those with the curiosity to listen and the heart to understand.

Gemma: (Entering the room) Jolie, you've got that determined look on your face again. What's going on?

Jolie: (Excitedly) You won't believe what I've discovered. I've been delving into the clock's past with the help of the town's historian.

Harley: (Curious) The clock's past? I thought we already knew about the tree and its magic.

Jolie: (Eagerly) But it's not just about the magic. It's about the people who were touched by it. Look at these old photographs and journals.

Gemma: (Looking at the photos) Wait, are these pictures of the tree being planted and the Boomer family, Kelly and Skippy?

The Whispering Secrets of Shinner House

Jolie: (Nodding) Yes, and that's not all. I learned that the tree's seed was brought back by our ancestors from one of their expeditions.

Harley: (Intrigued) So, the tree's magic dates back to their time?

Jolie: (Excited) Exactly! And it's not just our family – the tree had a profound impact on the people of this town. Look at these stories of love, dreams, and adventures in these journals.

Gemma: (Reading) "Married under the shade of the enchanted tree, their love blossomed like the leaves that whispered secrets."

Harley: (Flipping through the pages) "Embarked on a journey inspired by the tree's magic, discovering lands unknown and fulfilling dreams."

Jolie: (With awe) The tree's influence reaches beyond our family. It's like its magic spread throughout the town, touching lives in ways we never knew.

Gemma: (Reflective) The clock doesn't just hold our family's history; it holds the history of an entire community.

Harley: (Looking at the clock) And that's why it's so special. It's a bridge between generations, connecting us to the past and inspiring us for the future.

The Whispering Secrets of Shinner House

Jolie: (With determination) I want to share these stories with the town, to remind everyone of the magic that's been a part of this place for so long.

Gemma: (Supportive) You're right, Jolie. These stories deserve to be heard, to be celebrated.

Harley: (Dreamy) And just like the clock's melody, these stories will continue to echo through time.

Jolie: (Looking at her sisters) This house, this clock, they're not just ours. They belong to everyone who's been a part of their history.

Gemma: (Grinning) So, what's our next step, Jolie? How do we share these stories with the town?

Jolie: (Smiling) Together, as a family. Let's host an event, a gathering where we'll unveil the clock's stories and the gallery of Harley's enchanted paintings.

Harley: (Excited) A night of history, art, and magic – I love it.

Jolie: (Looking at the clock one last time) The clock's magic has brought us all closer, and now it's our turn to bring the community closer together.

The Whispering Secrets of Shinner House

With a shared vision and a renewed sense of purpose, the sisters embrace the task ahead, ready to weave the stories of the clock's magic into the fabric of their town's history.

Chapter 7

The Clock's Challenge

As the sisters delved deeper into the clock's magic, they realized that it was not only a source of wonder but also a guardian of the tree's legacy. It challenged them to use its powers responsibly and make wishes that would benefit the town. The clock's gentle reminders encouraged them to think beyond their personal desires.

The Whispering Secrets of Shinner House

As the days turned into weeks and the weeks into months, the bond between the sisters and the clock grew stronger, woven with threads of discovery, enchantment, and a shared purpose. They had come to understand that the clock was not merely a relic of the past or a wellspring of magic; it was a guardian of the tree's legacy, a bridge between the generations that had come before and the ones that would follow.

Through their individual journeys, Gemma, Harley, and Jolie had each uncovered facets of the clock's enchantment – the melodies that sang of history, the paintings that breathed with life, and the stories that whispered through time. Yet, they sensed that there was more to the clock's purpose than they had initially comprehended. Its melodies, while hauntingly beautiful, held a deeper resonance that went beyond their own desires.

One evening, as they gathered in the room with the clock, its melodies began to weave a new tune, one that stirred their hearts with a sense of responsibility. The notes were a gentle reminder, a subtle nudge from the clock's spirit that urged them to use its magic wisely, to make wishes that would benefit not just themselves but the entire town of Hutto.

The sisters exchanged knowing glances, recognizing the gravity of the clock's message. With its enchanting melodies as their guide, they embarked on a quest to uncover the ways in which they could make a positive impact on their community. They reached out to the townspeople, listening to their hopes, dreams, and aspirations.

Gemma, who had always been a natural leader, organized community gatherings where neighbors could share their stories and ideas. She discovered that many in the town wished for a revitalized park where families could gather, play, and create lasting memories. With the clock's gentle guidance, Gemma set her wish in motion, using its magic to infuse the park's construction with a sense of unity and harmony that would be felt for generations.

Harley, whose artistic spirit had been ignited by the clock's magic, realized that her gallery of enchanted paintings could serve as a source of inspiration for the town. She transformed her gallery into a community space, inviting artists of all ages to contribute their creations and share their stories. With the clock's encouragement, she wished for a vibrant arts center where imagination could flourish, and creativity could be nurtured.

Jolie, the keeper of stories and connections, found herself drawn to the town's elders, who held the memories of Hutto's history within their hearts. She organized storytelling sessions where the older generation shared tales of their youth, their families, and the town's evolution. With the clock's guidance, she wished for a community archive that would preserve these stories, ensuring that the legacy of Hutto would be passed down to future generations.

As their wishes came to fruition, the clock's melodies seemed to sing with a renewed sense of purpose. The sisters felt the tree's spirit watching over them, a benevolent presence that celebrated their efforts and encouraged them to continue using the clock's magic to create positive change. The town of Hutto began to flourish, its park bustling with laughter, its arts center alive with creativity, and its archive filled with cherished memories.

As time went on, the sisters realized that the clock's magic was not limited by its melodies or its enchanting aura. It reflected their own intentions, a catalyst for their dreams to take root and grow. The clock's gentle reminders continued, urging them to think beyond their personal desires and consider the greater good of their community.

And so, within the walls of Shinner House, where the clock's melodies and enchantment filled the air, Gemma, Harley, and Jolie learned that true magic went beyond the extraordinary abilities it granted. It resided in the choices they made, the wishes they nurtured, and the legacy they were crafting for the future. Through their connection with the clock, they discovered the profound impact that could be achieved when hearts were aligned with purpose and when magic was harnessed for the betterment of all.

The Whispering Secrets of Shinner House

Gemma: (Gathering with Harley and Jolie around the clock) Sisters, the more we learn about the clock's magic, the more I realize how powerful it truly is.

Jolie: (Nodding) It's not just about granting wishes. It's about safeguarding the tree's legacy and ensuring its magic is used responsibly.

Harley: (Thoughtful) The clock is like a guardian of the tree's essence, and we're its stewards.

Gemma: (Looking at the clock) Remember when it challenged us to think about the impact of our wishes on the town?

Jolie: (Recalling) Yeah, it's like the clock wants us to think beyond our personal desires and consider the greater good.

Harley: (Reflective) Our ancestors used the tree's magic to fulfill their dreams and aspirations, but they also used it to benefit the community.

Gemma: (Determined) We need to follow in their footsteps, to use the clock's powers to create positive change in the town.

The Whispering Secrets of Shinner House

Jolie: (With resolve) The clock's gentle reminders are guiding us to be responsible wish-makers.

Harley: (Smiling) So, no wishing for personal gain, but for the betterment of the community.

Gemma: (Looking at her sisters) Let's put our heads together and come up with wishes that would truly make a difference.

Jolie: (Thoughtful) Maybe we could wish for revitalizing the town square or bringing back a local tradition that's been forgotten.

Harley: (Eagerly) Or enhancing the local arts and culture scene, to inspire creativity in the generations to come.

Gemma: (Proud) I think our ancestors would be proud of us, carrying on their legacy of exploration and responsible use of magic.

Jolie: (Looking at the clock) The clock's magic is a gift, and with great power comes great responsibility.

Harley: (With determination) Let's make wishes that echo through time, just like the clock's melody.

Gemma: (Gazing at the clock with a sense of purpose) Shinner House and the clock have become more than just a part of our lives. They're part of the town's story, and we're writing the next chapter.

The Whispering Secrets of Shinner House

Jolie: (Smiling) And like every great story, it's not just about the magical elements; it's about the choices we make and the impact we leave behind.

Harley: (Linking arms with her sisters) To use the clock's magic for the greater good, for the heart of the town.

United by their commitment to the clock's legacy, the sisters stand together, ready to make wishes that will shape their community's future with a touch of enchantment.

Chapter 8

Uniting Wishes

With each sister understanding the clock's purpose, they decided to work together to make a wish that would honor the tree's history and impact the town positively. Their unity strengthened the clock's magic, and it began to emit a brilliant light that attracted the attention of the entire town.

The Whispering Secrets of Shinner House

With their individual journeys converging into a shared understanding, Gemma, Harley, and Jolie realized that the clock's magic reflected their collective intentions. The clock wasn't just a tool for personal desires; it was a beacon of unity, a vessel for the hopes and dreams of the past, present, and future. As they continued to explore its enchantment, they felt a profound connection to the tree's legacy and the town's history.

One evening, as the moon bathed Shinner House in a soft, silvery glow, the sisters gathered around the clock, their hearts aligned with a shared purpose. Their hands touched the clock's polished surface, and they closed their eyes, allowing their intentions to intertwine and mingle like threads of light. In that moment of unity, they whispered their wish — a wish that would honor the tree's history and positively impact the town of Hutto.

Their wish wasn't just for themselves or their family, but for the entire community that had supported them on their journey. It was a wish for prosperity, for unity, and for the enduring spirit of the deep South to flourish in the hearts of all who called Hutto home.

As the last echoes of their wish faded into the air, the clock seemed to respond. Its golden hands began to spin faster, its melodies melded into a symphony of harmonious notes, and a brilliant light emanated from its intricate carvings. The light swirled and danced, creating an aura that enveloped the room in a warm and enchanting glow.

The Whispering Secrets of Shinner House

Unbeknownst to the sisters, the brilliance of the clock's light extended beyond the walls of Shinner House. It spilled out into the night, casting its radiant glow across the town of Hutto. People stepped out of their homes, drawn by the ethereal light that painted the town square with shimmering hues of gold and silver.

The townspeople gathered in awe, their eyes fixed upon Shinner House as the clock's light pulsed like a heartbeat. The light seemed to reach out, touching the very souls of those who beheld it, filling them with a sense of wonder and unity. It was as though the clock's magic had awakened something deep within them, a connection to the past and a promise for the future.

Gemma, Harley, and Jolie opened their eyes, and their gaze met with the radiant light that emanated from the clock. Their hearts swelled with a mixture of awe and gratitude, for they knew that their wish had been heard and acknowledged by the ancient oak and the generations it had watched over.

As the clock's light continued to shine, a hushed silence fell over the town square. The moment was a testament to the power of unity, the magic of shared intentions, and the profound impact that individuals could have when their hearts beat in harmony. It was a moment that transcended time, a reminder that the tree's legacy was not just a tale of the past, but a living force that bound the people of Hutto together.

The Whispering Secrets of Shinner House

And so, within the heart of Shinner House and under the gaze of a brilliant light that illuminated the night, Gemma, Harley, and Jolie realized the true essence of the clock's enchantment. It was a gift that extended beyond the walls of their home, reaching into the lives and hearts of the entire town. Their shared wish had not only honored the tree's history but had also ignited a flame of hope and unity that would burn brightly for generations to come.

As the clock's light gradually dimmed, its melodies returned to their haunting beauty, resonating with a renewed sense of purpose. The sisters knew that their journey was far from over, that the magic of Shinner House and the ancient oak would continue to shape their lives and the lives of those who walked the path they had illuminated. And so, with hearts full of gratitude and anticipation, they embraced the legacy they were creating, guided by the clock's melodies, the tree's spirit, and the enduring magic of a place where dreams and history intertwined.

Gemma: (Gathering with Harley and Jolie in front of the clock) Sisters, it's time. We've delved into the clock's magic, and now we must use it responsibly.

The Whispering Secrets of Shinner House

Jolie: (Nodding) Agreed. We're not just making a wish for ourselves; we're making a wish that carries the weight of the tree's legacy and the town's hopes.

Harley: (Looking at the clock) The clock's gentle reminders have led us to this moment. Let's make a wish that truly honors its purpose.

Gemma: (With determination) We may each have our own dreams, but our wish should be a unity of our hearts, a reflection of the town's spirit.

Jolie: (Closing her eyes) As we make this wish, let's infuse it with the stories of the past and the aspirations of the future.

Harley: (Closing her eyes as well) May this wish echo through time, just like the clock's melody.

Gemma: (Closing her eyes) And may it light up the lives of the people in this town, just like the light that shines from the clock.

With their hearts united and their intentions clear, the sisters make their wish together. As they do, a brilliant light begins to emanate from the clock, filling the room and spilling out into the surrounding area.

The Whispering Secrets of Shinner House

Jolie: (Opening her eyes, amazed) Look at the light! It's like the clock is responding to our wish.

Harley: (In awe) It's as if the unity of our hearts has intensified the clock's magic.

Gemma: (Watching as the light extends beyond the room) Our wish is reaching out, touching every corner of the town.

Jolie: (Gazing at the light) This is a testament to the power of unity and the deep connection between us, the clock, and the town.

Harley: (With a sense of wonder) The clock's brilliance has caught the attention of the entire town. Everyone is coming this way.

Gemma: (With a smile) It's a reminder that we're all connected, that the heart of Shinner House and the clock beats within each one of us.

Jolie: (Looking at her sisters) Our unity has made the clock's magic stronger than ever. It's like the clock is saying that we're not just a family; we're a part of something greater.

Harley: (Feeling a sense of fulfillment) Our journey has come full circle. We've discovered the clock's purpose, made a wish that carries its legacy, and now the town is witnessing the magic we've uncovered.

The Whispering Secrets of Shinner House

Gemma: (Looking at the brilliant light) Our family's history, the clock's magic, and the town's hopes – they're all intertwined in this moment.

Jolie: (With gratitude) And it all started with a curiosity about an enchanted clock and a desire to uncover its secrets.

Harley: (Taking her sisters' hands) Sisters, as the light shines, let's remember this day and the power of unity and positive intention.

As the townspeople gather around, drawn by the light and the energy of the sisters' wish, a sense of awe and togetherness fills the air, reinforcing the bonds between the family, the clock, and the community.

Chapter 9

The Town's Transformation

As the clock's light spread across Hutto, the town underwent a magical transformation. Gardens flourished, the arts flourished, and kindness became the norm. The clock's enchantment helped people connect with their roots, fostering a sense of community and pride in their history.

The Whispering Secrets of Shinner House

As the radiant light from the clock spread across the town of Hutto, its transformative magic began to weave through every street, every home, and every heart. The impact of the sisters' shared wish was felt in every corner, touching lives, and reshaping the very essence of the community.

Gardens that had once been mere patches of soil burst forth with vibrant blooms and lush foliage. The plants seemed to respond to the clock's light, growing taller and more vibrant, their colors more vivid than ever before. As if guided by an invisible hand, people who had never before felt a connection to the earth found themselves drawn to gardening. Old and young alike embraced the joy of nurturing life, cultivating not just flowers, but a deep sense of renewal and growth.

The arts flourished in Hutto like never before. Inspired by the clock's enchantment, artists of all kinds stepped into the spotlight, their creativity fueled by the magic that seemed to infuse the air. Paintings, sculptures, music, and performances blossomed, reflecting the diverse voices and stories of the town. The arts became a bridge that connected people across generations, uniting them through shared expressions of beauty and imagination.

But it wasn't just the physical changes that marked the town's transformation; it was the way people treated one another. The magic of the clock's light seemed to ignite a spark of kindness and empathy within each person. Acts of generosity and compassion became a daily occurrence, as neighbors looked out for one another, strangers exchanged smiles and stories, and a sense of unity took root.

The clock's enchantment had a way of fostering connections with the past, sparking a newfound interest in the town's history and heritage. People delved into old books, photographs, and oral traditions, eager to uncover the stories that had shaped their town. The sense of pride in their history grew, as they realized that they were part of a rich tapestry woven with the threads of resilience, community, and the enduring spirit of the deep South.

Families gathered to share tales passed down through generations, strengthening the bonds that held them together. Elders found themselves surrounded by eager listeners, their memories cherished as living treasures. Younger generations learned to appreciate the lessons of the past and to carry them forward into the future.

As the clock's light continued to shine, the people of Hutto felt a deeper connection to the natural world around them. The whisper of the wind through the trees, the rustling of leaves, and the fragrance of blooming flowers became reminders of the ancient oak's presence and the magic it had shared with the town.

With each passing day, Hutto's transformation became more profound. It wasn't just a surface change – it was a shift in consciousness, a recognition of the interconnectedness of all things. The town had become a

The Whispering Secrets of Shinner House

living embodiment of the clock's magic, a place where the past, present, and future converged in a tapestry of wonder and unity.

Gemma, Harley, and Jolie watched with joy as their town flourished under the influence of the clock's enchantment. Their individual paths had converged into a shared purpose, and their journey had shaped not only their lives but the lives of everyone around them. With hearts full of gratitude and anticipation, they knew that the legacy they were building was one of love, connection, and the enduring magic of a place where dreams and history intertwined.

And so, within the heart of Hutto, where the clock's light illuminated the streets and the ancient oak's spirit danced in the wind, the town continued to thrive, guided by the wisdom of the past and the promise of the future. The enchantment of Shinner House had become a part of the town's very soul, a reminder that magic was not just a fleeting moment, but a force that could shape destinies and transform lives in ways beyond imagination.

The Whispering Secrets of Shinner House

Gemma: (Watching as the town bathes in the clock's light) Look at this, sisters. The town is undergoing a transformation right before our eyes.

Harley: (In awe) It's like the light is infusing life into every corner of Hutto.

Jolie: (Amazed) The gardens are flourishing, the colors are more vibrant, and there's a sense of joy in the air.

Gemma: (Smiling) And did you see the art installations that seemed to spring up overnight? The town's creativity is blooming too.

Harley: (Looking at the clock) The clock's magic isn't just about wishes; it's about making the town flourish in ways we couldn't have imagined.

Jolie: (Observing people interacting with each other) And did you notice how everyone seems to be more connected, more engaged?

Gemma: (With realization) It's like the clock's enchantment is helping people connect with their roots, with the town's history.

Harley: (Proudly) The stories we uncovered, the legacy of Shinner House, they're all playing a part in this transformation.

The Whispering Secrets of Shinner House

Jolie: (Looking at the clock's light) And the clock is reminding us that the heart of the town beats with the spirit of unity and kindness.

Gemma: (Reflective) The clock's magic has fostered a sense of community, pride in our history, and a commitment to a better future.

Harley: (With determination) Our ancestors' legacy, the clock's purpose, and our unity have all come together to shape this incredible change.

Jolie: (Feeling grateful) And we're a part of it. We're writing our own chapter in the town's story.

Gemma: (Looking at her sisters) Just like the clock's light, our impact is spreading far and wide, touching every person, every home.

Harley: (Gazing at the transformed town) It's like a dream, but it's real. The clock's enchantment has made a tangible difference.

Jolie: (Taking in the scene) Let's remember this moment, sisters. The night when our curiosity led us to uncover the magic that was already a part of our lives.

Gemma: (With a sense of fulfillment) The clock's light has ignited not only our town but also our own sense of purpose and connection.

The Whispering Secrets of Shinner House

Harley: (Looking at the clock one last time) The tree's legacy, the clock's magic, and our family's journey – they're all woven into the fabric of this town.

Jolie: (Taking her sisters' hands) As the clock's light continues to shine, let's keep nurturing this transformation and spreading the magic of unity, kindness, and pride.

The sisters stand together, watching as the town flourishes under the clock's enchantment, grateful for the role they played in shaping a brighter and more connected future.

Chapter 10

Embracing the Past and Future

As time went on, Gemma, Harley, and Jolie realized that the clock's magic was a reminder to cherish the past while embracing the future. The clock continued to whisper its stories and melodies, ensuring that the town's legacy would never be forgotten.

The Whispering Secrets of Shinner House

As the seasons turned and the years flowed like a river, the sisters – Gemma, Harley, and Jolie – continued to be stewards of the clock's magic and the legacy of Shinner House. With each passing day, their understanding of the clock's enchantment deepened, and the lessons it held became even more profound.

The clock, with its melodies and its stories, had taught them to honor the past, to treasure the threads that connected them to their ancestors, and to carry forward the wisdom that had been handed down through generations. The melodies whispered tales of love, adventure, and the resilience of those who had walked the paths of Hutto before them. The stories held lessons of triumphs and challenges, each thread woven into the tapestry of the town's history.

But the clock's magic was not just a relic of the past; it was a bridge that connected the past to the future. With each chime and every haunting melody, the clock reminded them that while the past held treasures to be cherished, the future was a canvas waiting to be painted with new stories, new dreams, and new adventures.

Gemma, as the eldest sister and a natural leader, spearheaded community projects that celebrated both the history and the potential of the town. She organized events that brought together people of all ages, from storytelling sessions that connected generations to festivals that celebrated Hutto's cultural diversity. The

The Whispering Secrets of Shinner House

clock's presence was felt in every gathering, a silent presence that served as a reminder of the deep well of wisdom from which the town drew its strength.

Harley, with her artistic soul, continued to inspire the town with her enchanting paintings. Her gallery expanded to include not only her own works but those of artists young and old who had been touched by the magic of Shinner House. Her paintings became visual stories of the town's evolution, capturing the essence of its history while also painting a picture of a future filled with hope and creativity.

Jolie, the keeper of stories, worked tirelessly to preserve the town's heritage. She curated a comprehensive archive that held the memories, photographs, and documents that told the story of Hutto's journey through time. The archive became a treasure trove for historians, researchers, and townspeople alike, a testament to the enduring power of the clock's enchantment.

As time went on, the sisters realized that the clock's magic was a constant companion, guiding them through the ebb and flow of life. Its melodies were a gentle reminder that the past was not something to be locked away, but a living force that shaped the present and inspired the future. Its stories were echoes that resounded across time, whispering tales of resilience, love, and the unbreakable spirit of a town that had weathered storms and celebrated triumphs.

The Whispering Secrets of Shinner House

The clock's melodies continued to weave their enchantment, resonating with a timeless rhythm that connected the sisters to their roots and propelled them towards the horizon. With every note, the clock whispered its message: to cherish the past while embracing the future, to honor the stories that had shaped them while creating new stories that would inspire generations to come.

And so, within the heart of Shinner House, where the clock's melodies and stories wove a tapestry of history and possibility, Gemma, Harley, and Jolie carried forward the legacy of the ancient oak and the enchantment it had bestowed upon their lives. With open hearts and minds, they looked towards the future, knowing that the magic of the clock would forever remind them of the beauty in embracing the past's wisdom while forging ahead into the uncharted territory of tomorrow.

Gemma: (Sitting with Harley and Jolie in the room with the clock) It's amazing how much has changed since we first discovered the clock's magic.

The Whispering Secrets of Shinner House

Harley: (Nodding) The town's transformation has been nothing short of magical, all thanks to the clock's enchantment.

Jolie: (Looking at the clock) And it's not just the town that's changed; we've changed too. Our perspective on the past and the future has shifted.

Gemma: (Reflective) The clock's magic is like a bridge between generations, reminding us to cherish our history while embracing the possibilities of the future.

Harley: (Smiling) It's a reminder that the past isn't just something to preserve; it's something to learn from, to be inspired by.

Jolie: (Listening to the clock's melody) And the melodies that the clock whispers, they're like echoes of the stories it holds.

Gemma: (Looking at the clock) Those stories are a part of our family's legacy, but they're also a part of the town's soul.

Harley: (Thoughtful) The clock's melodies are a continuation of the history it carries, ensuring that the legacy lives on.

Jolie: (Feeling a sense of connection) And as we listen to those melodies, we're connecting with the people who came before us, the ones who loved and dreamed under the tree's shade.

The Whispering Secrets of Shinner House

Gemma: (Gazing at the clock's face) It's a reminder that we're a part of something bigger, a tapestry woven with the threads of the past and the threads of the future.

Harley: (Taking in the room's atmosphere) And just like the clock's melodies, our lives are like notes that add to the symphony of this town's story.

Jolie: (With a sense of contentment) The clock's magic has become a part of our lives, a guiding presence that encourages us to keep moving forward while holding onto our roots.

Gemma: (Closing her eyes, listening to the clock) The clock is whispering its stories even now, reminding us that the town's legacy will never be forgotten.

Harley: (Feeling a sense of gratitude) Our journey has been a blend of adventure, discovery, and a touch of enchantment.

Jolie: (With a smile) And it's a journey that we'll carry with us, just like the clock's melodies will always echo in our hearts.

Gemma: (Linking arms with her sisters) As the clock continues to tick, let's continue to cherish our past while embracing the limitless possibilities of the future.

The Whispering Secrets of Shinner House

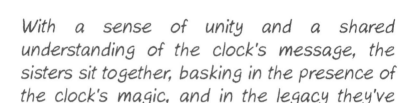

With a sense of unity and a shared understanding of the clock's message, the sisters sit together, basking in the presence of the clock's magic, and in the legacy they've created for their town and their family.

Chapter 11

A Lasting Legacy

Years passed, and the sisters grew old, passing on the legacy of the enchanted clock to the next generation. The tree's spirit lived on; its magic woven into the fabric of Hutto's identity. The town flourished, always remembering the sisters' story and the lessons of unity, creativity, and responsibility that the enchanted clock had taught them.

The Whispering Secrets of Shinner House

Years flowed gracefully, like the pages of a well-worn book, as the sisters – Gemma, Harley, and Jolie – grew old with the weight of time's passage. Their hair turned silver, their steps became slower, but their spirits remained as vibrant as ever. They had become living legends, their stories interwoven with the history of Hutto, an indelible part of the tapestry of the town's identity.

As the sisters entered a new chapter of their lives, they felt a profound sense of contentment and fulfillment. They had dedicated their years to nurturing the magic of the clock and fostering the bonds of community. Now, it was time to pass on the legacy they had cultivated to the next generation – a generation that would carry forward the lessons of unity, creativity, and responsibility that the enchanted clock had taught them.

Gemma, with her wisdom and leadership, gathered the town's youth to share the tales of the clock, its melodies, and the transformative journey she, her sisters, and the town had undertaken. She spoke of the importance of cherishing history and embracing change, encouraging them to be stewards of the clock's magic and guardians of Hutto's heritage.

Harley, with her artistic spirit undimmed, continued to create breathtaking paintings that captured the essence of Hutto's past and the dreams of its future. She mentored young artists, passing on the techniques and the message that creativity was a force that could shape reality. Her

The Whispering Secrets of Shinner House

gallery became a source of inspiration and a living testament to the enduring power of the clock's enchantment.

Jolie, now the town's cherished historian, documented the passing of time with the same meticulous dedication she had applied to preserving history. She mentored apprentices who would carry the torch of storytelling forward, ensuring that the stories of Hutto's journey remained alive for generations to come. Her archive grew, a treasure trove that held the collective memories of a town bound by the magic of the clock.

As the sisters gently handed over the stewardship of the clock's legacy, the town embraced its role with reverence. The tree's spirit, though unseen, was ever-present, its magic woven into the very fabric of Hutto's identity. The town's gardens flourished, not only with vibrant flora but with the blossoms of creativity and compassion. The arts continued to thrive, as the community celebrated the unique talents of its members. Acts of kindness became the norm, a testament to the lasting influence of the clock's enchantment.

Through the passing years, Hutto continued to flourish, a living testament to the sisters' journey and the lessons they had imparted. The town's streets remained lined with the blossoms that had once caught Jolie's eye, a reminder of the beauty that could be found in the everyday. The clock's melodies continued to sing, resonating with a sense

The Whispering Secrets of Shinner House

of timelessness that connected the past, present, and future.

The story of the sisters and the enchanted clock became woven into the very heartbeat of Hutto. The town's children grew up listening to the tales, their imaginations sparked by the magic that seemed to linger in the air. Families gathered around the clock, sharing stories of their ancestors and the ways in which the clock had touched their lives.

And so, as the sun set on the lives of Gemma, Harley, and Jolie, their legacy endured. The tree's spirit whispered through the leaves, the clock's melodies echoed through the ages, and the lessons of unity, creativity, and responsibility continued to shape the town's destiny. Hutto, now a thriving community bound by the bonds of the past and the promise of the future, carried the enchantment of the clock within its very soul, a living testament to the enduring magic of a place where dreams, history, and the human spirit intertwined.

Gemma: (Sitting on a bench in Shinner House's garden, looking at the clock) How time has flown, sisters. We've seen the town change and flourish, and now we're passing on the legacy.

Harley: (Sitting beside Gemma) It warms my heart to see the generations that have come after us, embracing the clock's magic and the lessons it holds.

Jolie: (Joining them) The tree's spirit lives on, and so does the unity, creativity, and responsibility that the clock taught us.

Gemma: (Nodding) The clock has become more than just a timekeeper; it's become a symbol of our family's journey and the town's identity.

Harley: (Smiling) And it's still whispering its melodies, still telling stories that remind everyone of our shared history.

Jolie: (Looking around at the gardens and the bustling town) Hutto has become a living testament to the clock's magic and the impact it's had on all of us.

Gemma: (With a sense of fulfillment) Our chapter in this story may be ending, but the legacy we've left behind will continue to inspire.

Harley: (Watching children play near the clock) Just like we were drawn to the clock all those years ago, the next generations will be drawn to its enchantment.

Jolie: (Feeling grateful) And they'll carry forward the values we've learned – unity, creativity, responsibility.

The Whispering Secrets of Shinner House

Gemma: (Looking at the clock's face) As we grow old, the clock remains a constant, a reminder of the journey we've taken and the impact we've made.

Harley: (Squeezing Gemma's hand) And it's a reminder that our story, the story of the clock, and the story of Hutto are all intertwined.

Jolie: (With a sense of contentment) Our lives have been woven into the fabric of this town's identity, and it's a privilege to see it thrive.

Gemma: (Closing her eyes, listening to the clock's melody) The clock's melodies continue to guide us, even as we reflect on our past and the path that lies ahead.

Harley: (Smiling at Jolie) The clock's magic has become a legacy we can be proud of, a story that's touched so many lives.

Jolie: (Looking at the clock's gentle glow) And as we pass on the responsibility to the next generation, let's trust that they'll honor the clock's purpose just as we did.

The Whispering Secrets of Shinner House

With a sense of peace and a shared understanding of the passage of time, the sisters sit together, their bond as strong as ever, as they pass on the legacy of the enchanted clock to the future generations of Hutto.

The Whispering Secrets of Shinner House

Epilogue

The Eternal Melody

Even now, the clock's melody can be heard on moonlit nights, carrying the whispers of the past and the dreams of the future. The enchanted grandfather clock remains a symbol of Hutto's enduring magic, reminding all who hear its song to listen to the secrets of the heart and the stories of the ages.

The Whispering Secrets of Shinner House

Even in the embrace of the present, the echoes of the past and the dreams of the future are interwoven into the fabric of Hutto's existence. As moonlit nights cast a silvery glow upon the town, a haunting melody drifts through the air – the ethereal song of the enchanted grandfather clock. Its chimes resound through the stillness, a gentle reminder that time is a bridge that spans generations, carrying with it the whispers of the past and the aspirations of the future.

The clock's melodies are a portal, transporting listeners to a realm where history and possibility merge. Those who listen closely can hear the laughter of couples twirling beneath the ancient oak's branches, the rustle of pages turning in dusty journals, and the heartbeat of a town united by the bonds of community. It's as if the clock's enchantment allows time to fold upon itself, inviting all who hear its song to become part of the grand tapestry of Hutto's story.

The clock has become more than just a timekeeper; it is a living testament to the enduring magic that resides in the heart of the town. Its melodies are a bridge to the past, a melody that sings of love, resilience, and the unwavering spirit of those who have called Hutto home. The stories of the sisters – Gemma, Harley, and Jolie – have become entwined with the clock's legacy, a reminder of their journey and the lessons they learned about unity, creativity, and responsibility.

The Whispering Secrets of Shinner House

As townspeople and visitors alike pause to listen to the clock's melody, they find themselves transported through time. The whispers of the past become a call to action in the present, encouraging all to be stewards of the town's heritage and to contribute to the dreams that will shape the future. The clock's song serves as a reminder that each individual is part of a larger narrative, a continuation of a story that has been unfolding for generations.

The enchanted grandfather clock remains a symbol of Hutto's enduring magic, standing as a sentinel to the town's history and a beacon of hope for what is yet to come. Its intricate carvings and polished wood hold within them the essence of a place where dreams, history, and the human spirit intertwine. It beckons all who hear its song to listen not only to the melodies that dance through the night but to the secrets of their own hearts and the stories of the ages that live within them.

And so, under the moonlit sky, where the clock's melody weaves its enchanting spell and the ancient oak's spirit lingers in the breeze, Hutto remains a place of wonder and inspiration. The legacy of the sisters and the clock lives on, reminding all who hear its song that they are part of a timeless tale, where the past and the future unite in a symphony of hope, love, and the enduring magic of a place where dreams find their home.

The Whispering Secrets of Shinner House

Gemma: (Sitting on a porch swing, looking at the moonlit night) It's a beautiful night, just like the ones when we first discovered the clock's melody.

Harley: (Sitting beside Gemma) The clock's song still fills the air, carrying the whispers of stories and dreams.

Jolie: (Joining them) It's a reminder that the magic of Shinner House and the clock will never fade.

Gemma: (Listening to the melody) The clock's song is a bridge between the past and the future, a constant reminder of our journey.

Harley: (Smiling) And it's a reminder that our story, the clock's story, and the town's story are all woven together.

Jolie: (With a sense of wonder) The clock's melody has become a part of the town's heartbeat, a source of comfort and inspiration.

Gemma: (Looking at the clock in the moonlight) It's like the clock is a guardian of Hutto's enduring magic, a magic that transcends time.

Harley: (Closing her eyes, listening to the melody) The clock's song carries the secrets of the heart and the stories of generations.

The Whispering Secrets of Shinner House

Jolie: (Reflecting) And even as the years pass, its melody remains a reminder to cherish the past and embrace the dreams of the future.

Gemma: (With a sense of contentment) Our lives, our choices, and the clock's magic have all contributed to the legacy we see and hear tonight.

Harley: (Taking a deep breath) It's a legacy that will continue to touch lives, just like it touched ours.

Jolie: (Feeling a sense of gratitude) And as the clock's melody echoes through time, it's a reminder that our journey, like the clock's song, is a melody of its own.

Gemma: (Looking at her sisters) Our story, the clock's story, they're all part of the symphony of life that continues to play on.

Harley: (Squeezing Gemma's hand) As the clock's melody weaves through the night, let's remember that our journey has been a melody worth sharing.

Jolie: (Listening to the clock's melody) And as we listen, let's know that our legacy lives on, carried by the whispers of the past and the dreams of the future.

The Whispering Secrets of Shinner House

With a sense of unity and a shared understanding of the enduring magic they've left behind, the sisters sit together, embracing the timeless connection they have with the enchanted grandfather clock and the town of Hutto.

Sadly, This Brings Us To The End
Of Our Enchanted Story...

Or Does It ? Tic...Toc...
Sleep Tight...

Made in the USA
Monee, IL
03 September 2023

42054809R00056